# Liam and the Lizard

by Peta-Gaye Nash

Illustrated by Anindita Modak

Published by

IQWI

Liam and the Lizard
Written by:      Peta-Gaye Nash
Published by:    In Our Words Inc.
                 inourwords.ca
Illustrated by:  Anindita Modak
Layout Design:   Shirley Aguinaldo

Library and Archives Canada Cataloguing in Publication
 Nash, Peta-Gaye
      Liam and the Lizard / Peta-Gaye Nash.

ISBN 978-1-926926-14-8


      1. Title.


PS8627.A776L53 2011          jC813'.6          C2011-907551-2

# Dedication

**Liam and Lucas**
P.N.


**Maa, Baba, Sanjib and my bro John**
A.M.

Liam was born in Canada but his parents are Jamaican, so for the Christmas vacation he went to Jamaica to visit his relatives who still live there.

Jamaica and Canada are like two very different worlds. The biggest difference is that in December, Canada is cold and sometimes snow covers the ground. In Jamaica however, December is hot. So Liam went swimming almost every day, even on Christmas Day.

Another difference is that unlike Canada, there are many lizards in Jamaica. Liam wanted to catch one, but they always ran away.  Some lizards were flat and white, while others were small and brown.

Liam wanted to hold one in his hand. He really wanted a lizard for a pet.

So Liam asked his Grandpa Peter for help.

"Grandpa Peter, can you help me catch a lizard?"

"Sure, but I have a bad back. I'll help as soon as I'm feeling better."

Grandpa Peter didn't seem to feel any better so Liam asked his older cousin Jason.

"Can you help me catch a lizard?"

"Sure," said Jason, "but that one is too high. Let's wait until he comes down."

The lizard didn't want to come down. It remained high up on the wall near the ceiling for the entire day.

Liam went to find his Great-Grandma Mavis to ask her to help him.

"Grandma Mavis, there's a lizard on your wall. Can you help me catch him?"

"A lizard? Where? My house has screen doors and windows to keep out pests. What's he doing in here?"

Then his Great-Grandma Mavis ran to the kitchen and came back with a broom to scare the lizard away.

"I'm going to fix his business if he ever comes here again," she muttered under her breath.

Liam asked his Grandma Jenny if she could help him catch a lizard.

"Oooh, not me, honey. I don't like them. Ask your Grandpa Ernie."

"Grandpa Ernie, can you help me catch a lizard?"

"A lizard? I can try, but after I finish cooking."

Grandpa Ernie was in the kitchen for a long time and by the time he came out, it was too dark.

Liam asked everyone to help him catch a lizard but no one seemed to be able to help him.

Then the day before Liam left Jamaica to go back to Canada, his Great-Grandma Madge gave him a gift. It was a little matchbox with a tiny baby lizard inside.

"You can't take him back to Canada but you can play with him here. I caught him for you," she said.

Everyone was astonished to hear her say that.

"I can't believe it," said Auntie Anji. "She must love Liam very much. You know she has been terrified of lizards ever since she was a child when her brother Neville put a lizard in her hair."

"Yuk!" gasped Liam's mommy. "That's terrible."

"Yes," agreed Auntie Anji. "That's why I can't believe she caught a lizard for Liam."

Liam really loved his lizard. He named him Little Dinosaur. He didn't want to go back to Canada without him and besides, he wanted to show Little Dinosaur to all his friends at school for Show-and-Tell.

He put Little Dinosaur in his jeans pocket and went to the airport.  Then he went through customs and immigration and right onto the plane.

No one knew he had Little Dinosaur with him.

The plane was crowded. Liam wasn't able to sit beside mommy. She was behind him reading a magazine.  Liam sat quietly between a woman and his daddy who was beside him, but asleep and snoring.

The woman sitting beside Liam looked very serious and sad. Liam wanted to cheer her up.

"Would you like to meet my friend?" he asked her.

"Who is your friend, little boy?"

Liam reached into his pocket and took out the matchbox and opened it. Little Dinosaur stared up at the woman.

"Lawd, help me," screamed the woman, throwing her hands up into the air. "Lawd, have mercy on me."

She tried to jump up but she forgot she was wearing a seatbelt. Her hands were waving wildly and she knocked the matchbox out of Liam's hands. Little Dinosaur flew out of the box and landed on a woman's head. The woman jumped out of her seat and shook her head wildly.

"Somebody call 911. Call 911. Lizard on my head!" she screamed.

The man who was sitting beside her jumped up and onto someone's lap.

"Help!" he screamed hugging the stranger in whose lap he was sitting. "I'm terrified of lizards. Don't let the lizard get me."

Liam couldn't understand all the commotion. The lizard was as tiny as his mommy's little finger and the entire planeload of people seemed to be screaming in fright. Even the flight attendants seemed a little jumpy as they ran around trying to catch Little Dinosaur.

"Don't hurt Little Dinosaur," shouted Liam. "He's my friend and I'm taking him back to Canada. He's going to live with me."

"Honey, Little Dinosaur can't live in Canada," said Liam's mommy. "It's too cold. He needs the warm sun all the time. He needs to be outside with all his friends. He'll be lonely in Canada. There won't be any other lizards for him to play with."

Liam started to cry.

"But I love Little Dinosaur. I want to stay with him in Jamaica."

Daddy put Liam on his lap and hugged him.

Then the pilot came out looking very stern.

"What's all the commotion?" he asked.

"This little boy brought a lizard on the plane," said a woman pointing to Liam. "This is an emergency. You must land the plane now and get the lizard out."

"Ma'am, I can't land the plane in the middle of the ocean," said the pilot pointing out the window. "Please sit down and be calm."

Finally a passenger caught Little Dinosaur.

"Here's the little fellow. He was hiding in my jacket."

"In your jacket?" screamed the woman sitting beside Liam. Then she fainted.

Liam took Little Dinosaur and put him back in the matchbox.

"Don't let him out again," said the man sitting on the passenger's lap, in a trembling voice.

"I'm sorry son, but he has to go back to Jamaica," said the pilot taking the matchbox from Liam.

"But why?" cried Liam.

"Lizards are cold-blooded. That means that if the weather is cold they will be cold and if the weather is warm they will stay warm. If it's too cold they can't move. I think Little Dinosaur will be happier where it's warm and where he has friends like him."

Liam started to cry again.

"I'll tell you what," said the pilot. "After this plane flies to Canada, it's going to turn around and fly right back to Jamaica. I'll take Little Dinosaur home for you."

"Do you promise?" asked Liam.

"I promise."

"Are you scared of him?"

"No," smiled the pilot. "I'm not scared. I promise I won't hurt him. He can come with me into the cockpit and fly all the way back to Jamaica."

"Okay," said Liam, smiling and drying his tears.

Liam turned to his mommy. "Can I get an iguana for a pet when we go back to Canada?"

"An iguana! Lawd have mercy!" exclaimed the woman sitting beside Liam. Then she fainted again.

When the plane landed in Toronto, Liam said goodbye to Little Dinosaur and kissed him gently on his back. He gave the lizard to the pilot.

The pilot kept his promise. When he got back to Jamaica, he took Little Dinosaur out of the matchbox and put him down near a tree with large orange flowers.

"Bye, little fellow," he said as Little Dinosaur scurried off into the bushes.

As for Liam, his mommy and daddy took him to a pet store.

"I can't decide if I want an iguana or a snake," said Liam.

"A snake?" said mommy. "Oh no!"

Finally they all decided on turtles. And so Liam finally got a pet.